This book belongs to:

....

With love for Grandma Margaret.
– A.S.

To my family who provide me with an umbrella of support
and to my students who become giddy on rainy days.

With thanks to K.G. for her editing help and patience.
–J.L.

First published in 2009 by Simply Read Books
www.simplyreadbooks.com

Library and Archives Canada Cataloguing in Publication

Lloyd, Jennifer
    Ella's umbrellas / Jennifer Lloyd ; Ashley Spires, illustrator.

ISBN 978-1-897476-23-9
    I. Spires, Ashley, 1978- II. Title.

PS8623.L69E55 2009   jC813'.6   C2009-901957-4

We gratefully acknowledge for their financial support of our publishing program the Canada Council for the Arts, the BC Arts Council, and the Government of Canada through the Book Publishing Industry Development Program (BPIDP).

Book design by Grace Partridge

10 9 8 7 6 5 4 3 2 1

Manufactured by Tien Wah Press
Manufactured in Singapore, Sept, 2009
Job # : 32769

Ella's Umbrellas

BY Jennifer Lloyd

ILLUSTRATIONS BY Ashley Spires

SIMPLY READ BOOKS

*E*lla had big umbrellas and small umbrellas.
She had umbrellas in pink, turquoise and tangerine.
She had them in every color, even jellybean green.

Several were striped and a few speckled with spots.
A sprinkling had sparkles. A handful had hearts.
Some opened slowly and plenty went POP!

Ella had too many umbrellas.

It was not her fault. Her family and friends knew
that she loved umbrellas. So when she received a gift,
it was undoubtedly an umbrella.

Out of them all, Ella's favorite was robin's egg blue.
It came from someone special: kind Aunt Stella
from far-off Kathmandu.

To Ella's delight, Stella was coming to visit that very day.
And she was going to stay in Ella's room!

Ella's mother was usually patient, but today she was in a tizzy.

"Ella!" she cried. "Aunt Stella will have no place to hang her coat! Aunt Stella will have no place to put her clothes! Aunt Stella will have no place to sleep!"

Ella tried to fix the problem:

She tidied the coat closet ... and cluttered the kitchen sink!

She emptied her bedroom closet ... and filled the bathtub!

She cleared off
the bottom bunk ...
and loaded the
dishwasher!

"Ella!" cried her mother. "Your umbrellas
are everywhere! You have so many.
There are people in this world that
don't have any. You must find a way
to give your umbrellas away."

Give her umbrellas away? Ella hesitated. But, seeing
her mother's scowl, she gathered them all up.

She tossed them into a humongous heap in the front yard.
The blue from Kathmandu she kept safely by her side.
She made a teeny tiny sign that said, "Free Umbrellas."

In the distance, Ella heard the postman whistling.

He came near, but he didn't reach for an umbrella.
Instead he handed Ella a postcard.

Dear Ella,

See you soon!

Love,
Aunt Stella

For: Ella

Ella twiddled her thumbs and waited

and waited

and waited ...

Vrooooom!

Until her mother came out to mow the lawn. She spotted the tiny sign on the mountain of umbrellas.

"Ella!" she cried. "You have too many umbrellas!
You must find a better way to give them away!"

Ella slowly made a bigger sign.
She piled the umbrellas into her
wagon but held tight to the blue
from Kathmandu.

Lugging her load towards town, she did not notice
the creeping clouds all around. The wind came up.
It started to sprinkle. The rain grew heavier . . . *and heavier!*

Soon it was a TORRENTIAL DOWNPOUR!

PITTER! PATTER! SPLASH!

A wet jogger slowed down and gazed hopefully at
Ella's wagon. To her surprise, he didn't take an umbrella.
Ella examined her sign. She stared at her too many
umbrellas, then at the sad, soggy jogger.

"Wait!" she shouted. "Take this."

"Thank you," he said, happily
bobbing off on his way.

SPLISH! SPLASH!
A boy on a scooter was rushing
through puddles.
"Can I have one?" he yelled.

"Of course!"

Ella felt proud. She had given away two.
Quite enough, she decided. She turned towards home.

But on her way back she met a cold crossing guard and dripping day camp children. She met a drenched dog walker and waterlogged workmen – all without umbrellas.

Each time she gave one away she felt a tiny bit sad. But deep down she also felt glad. Soon, only her favorite umbrella remained. Surely her mother wouldn't mind if she kept just this one.

Still a few streets from home, Ella saw
a figure plodding down the sidewalk.

His blue cap was drenched. His sack looked heavy.
And he certainly wasn't whistling.

It was very hard, but Ella knew what to do.

Back at home, a suitcase sat by the door.

"Aunt Stella!" yelled Ella, leaping into her arms.

"Ella!" boomed her aunt, handing her a long, thin box.

Inside, in bright emerald green, was the most precious umbrella Ella had ever seen.